CHRIS

JENNY

To my love, J.D., and our children, Olivia, Ethan, Gavin, and Braden. You're my inspiration behind GRIT. I love you all. To my parents, Tom and Janice, and sisters, Julie and Jill. Having friends that are family is a wonderful gift. To Bryce, Brooks, Cole, Elinor, Edwin, and Jesse, never forget that Aunt Jen Jen is here for you. Lastly, thank you to my DVB family for introducing me to the construction world.

CHRIS

To Hale, Sadie, and Kennan for making me want to be a better person. To the DVB team for always keeping me on my toes and teaching me so much. Special thanks to Sarah for getting us to the finish line. To you, I hope you follow your dreams, seek adventure, inspire others, and remember that Grit Leads to Greatness.

MASCOT KIDS!
an imprint of Amplify Publishing Group

mascotbooks.com

GRIT LEADS TO GREATNESS

For more information, please contact:
Mascot Kids, an imprint of Amplify Publishing Group
620 Herndon Parkway #320
Herndon, VA 20170
info@mascotbooks.com

Commemorative First Edition: Advanced Digital Print • February 2023

Library of Congress Control Number: 2023932099

ISBN-13: 978-1-63755-531-6

Printed in the United States

GritLeadsToGreatness.com

GRIT LEADS TO GREATNESS

An Epic Quest Built To Change THE World

BY **JENNY KERR SCHROEN** AND **CHRIS ECCLESTON**

Illustrated by **Justin Donaldson** with **Rachel Danae**

There once was a vibrant city with grand structures, beautiful parks, and stately statues perched on an impossibly steep mountainside.

Long ago, glowing stones, which mysteriously appeared in the town, hypnotized anyone who gazed upon them. The people's obsession become so powerful that over time, the majestic city was neglected, its buildings slowly

Brother and sister Trig and Tegan were different from most kids. They believed there had to be more to life than the glowing stones. Instead, they explored the world around them.

Day after day the siblings played next to the statues positioned along the main boulevard. They would make up fantastic stories of what people had achieved to gain the honor of having their likeness carved out of marble.

One afternoon while the two were playing, a piece of a crumbling statue fell, nearly crushing Trig. Out of nowhere, an old man rescued the boy from impending death.

GRIT LEADS TO GREATNESS

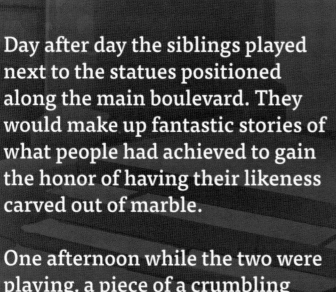

As Tegan helped them to their feet, she recognized it was Ohm, the same feeble man known for his thick glasses, who could usually be found at the city center

Looking down the line of broken statues, Ohm told the kids, "These people found Greatness." This got Tegan and Trig's attention.

"Greatness is where people use their abilities and experiences to change the world."

He went on to explain. "It's an incredible place, but the journey is not easy. Most people give up on finding Greatness because it can't be found without the power of GRIT."

Puzzled, Tegan questioned Ohm. **"What is GRIT?"**

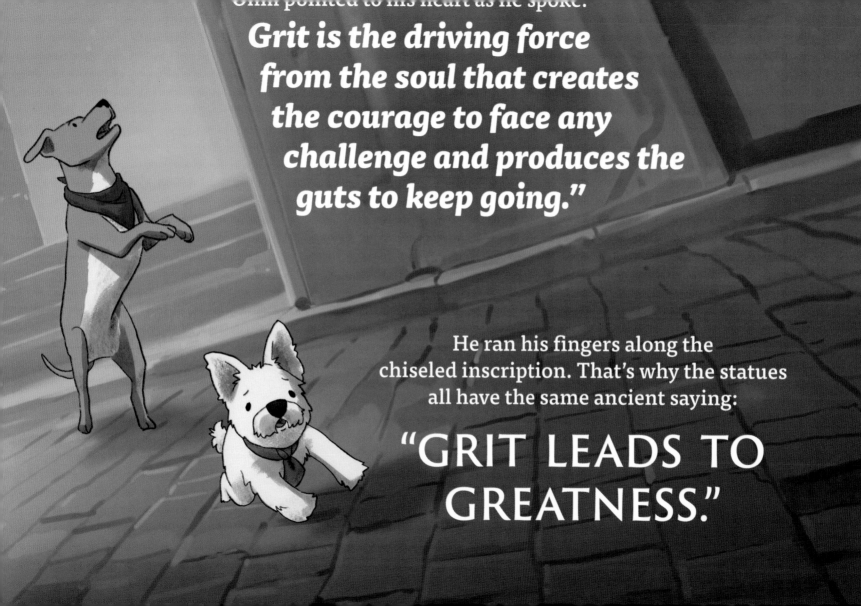

Uhm pointed to his heart as he spoke.

Grit is the driving force from the soul that creates the courage to face any challenge and produces the guts to keep going.

He ran his fingers along the chiseled inscription. That's why the statues all have the same ancient saying:

"GRIT LEADS TO GREATNESS."

Frightened, the people rushed to the town center. There, they received a dire warning from Ohm: "The city will fall if someone doesn't repair the cracked supports!" Not one person in the crowd knew what to do. Many continued to grip their glowing stones, pretending they never heard the terrible news.

The siblings locked eyes. Their encounter with Ohm was no coincidence.

Did they even have this thing called GRIT?

Was the saying even true?

There were so many questions.

"The truth is, no one's coming to our rescue," Tegan stated as Trig spotted the old man near the statues.

Ohm's head was in his palms as Trig shook him desperately. "How do we find Greatness? Someone there must be able to help us." Looking up, Ohm reached into his coat pocket, producing a map.

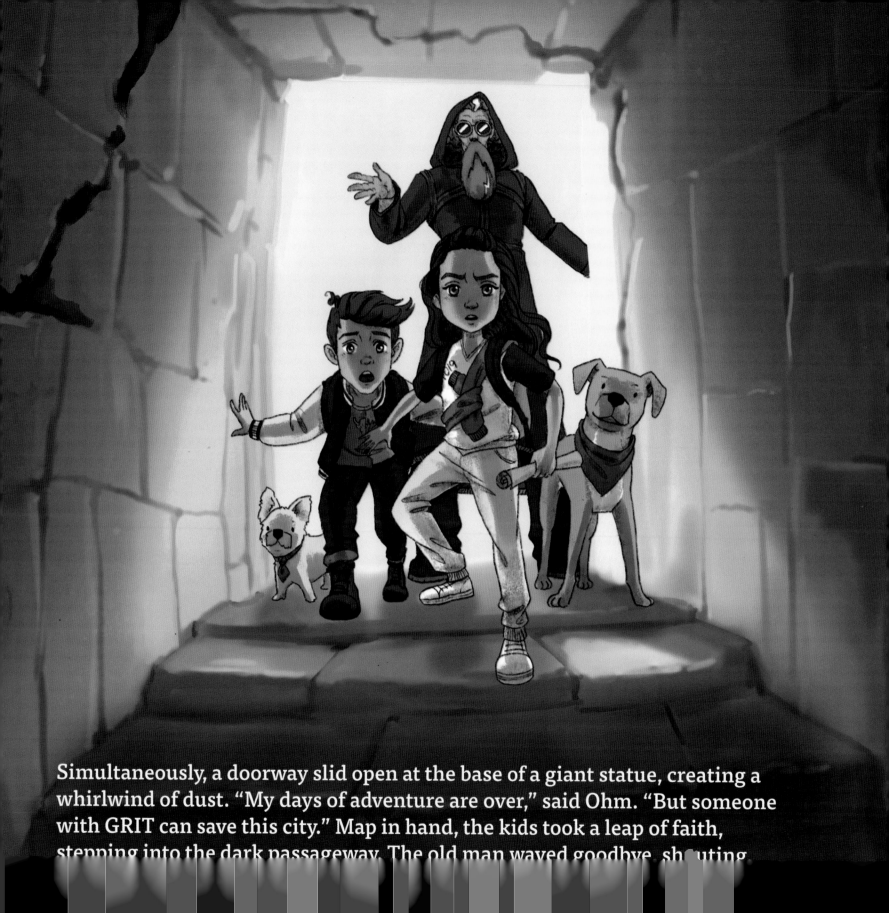

Simultaneously, a doorway slid open at the base of a giant statue, creating a whirlwind of dust. "My days of adventure are over," said Ohm. "But someone with GRIT can save this city." Map in hand, the kids took a leap of faith, stepping into the dark passageway. The old man waved goodbye, shouting,

As they exited the long tunnel, the landscape
became a rough, rocky terrain. Before them stood
a dignified Ogre carrying a boulder, who seemed
shocked to see them. "It's been thousands of years since
I've seen people walk this path," declared the giant.

The kids were not sure what to think. Weren't Ogres supposed
to be unintelligent?

"My friends call me Mason the Mason. I am a tradesperson—a worker of
stone. We've cut back the mountainside to build a retaining wall, providing
travelers a safe route up the mountain. Unfortunately, the trail will be
blocked until we finish."

"But this path leads to Greatness!" Trig groaned.

"We either give up and go home, or we stay and help build the wall," declared Tegan. They both knew there was too much at stake to turn back.

Ready to work, the kids eagerly accepted a trowel from Mason. Concrete footers were poured deep into the earth while they learned the skills needed to lay block. He explained the engineering required to withstand the forces of nature as the trio mortared the wall higher and higher.

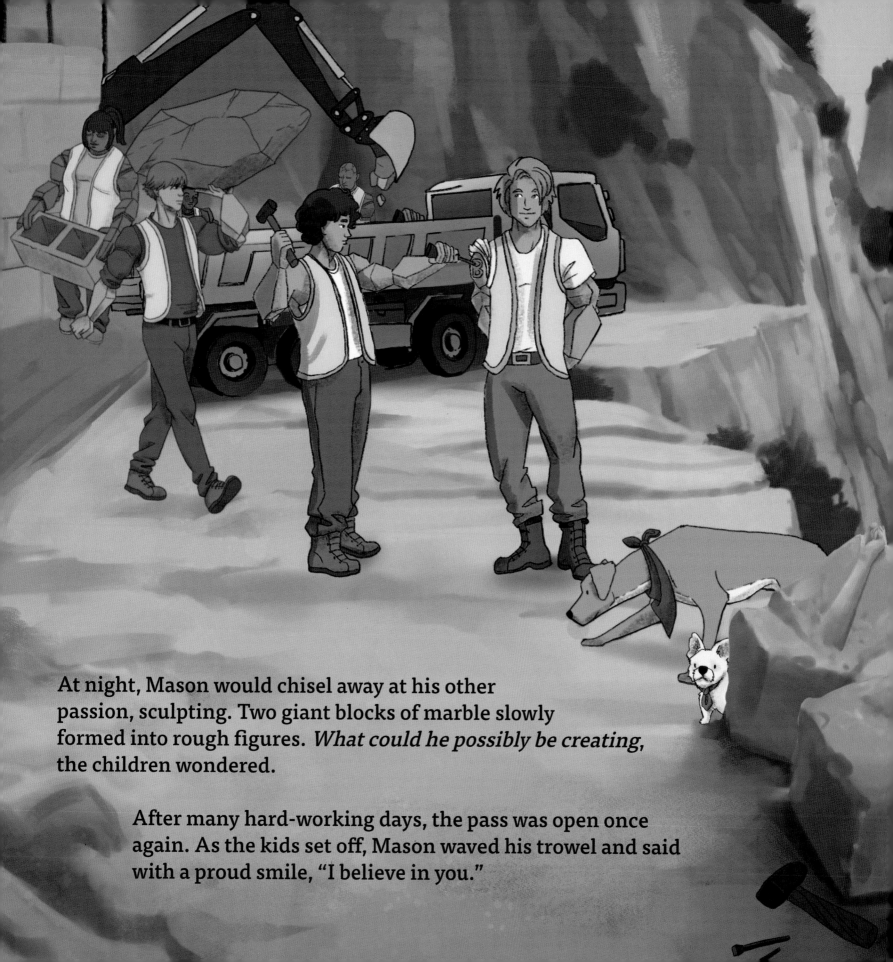

At night, Mason would chisel away at his other passion, sculpting. Two giant blocks of marble slowly formed into rough figures. *What could he possibly be creating,* the children wondered.

After many hard-working days, the pass was open once again. As the kids set off, Mason waved his trowel and said with a proud smile, "I believe in you."

Their path turned to ice as the siblings wound their way up the treacherous pass.

Through the snow-covered trees appeared a tiny village, bustling with little figures skiing, snowboarding, and lounging in steamy, blue lagoons. It looked like a magical winter wonderland.

Trig felt a tug on his pant leg. Smiling up at him, the miniature person introduced herself. "My name is Rowan. We're Snomes, carpenters by trade, who use the trees to construct lodges, build furniture, and carve wood."

She led the kids to a large construction site where there was a
flurry of Snomes sawing and moving timber. Rowan explained
they were building a much-needed school.

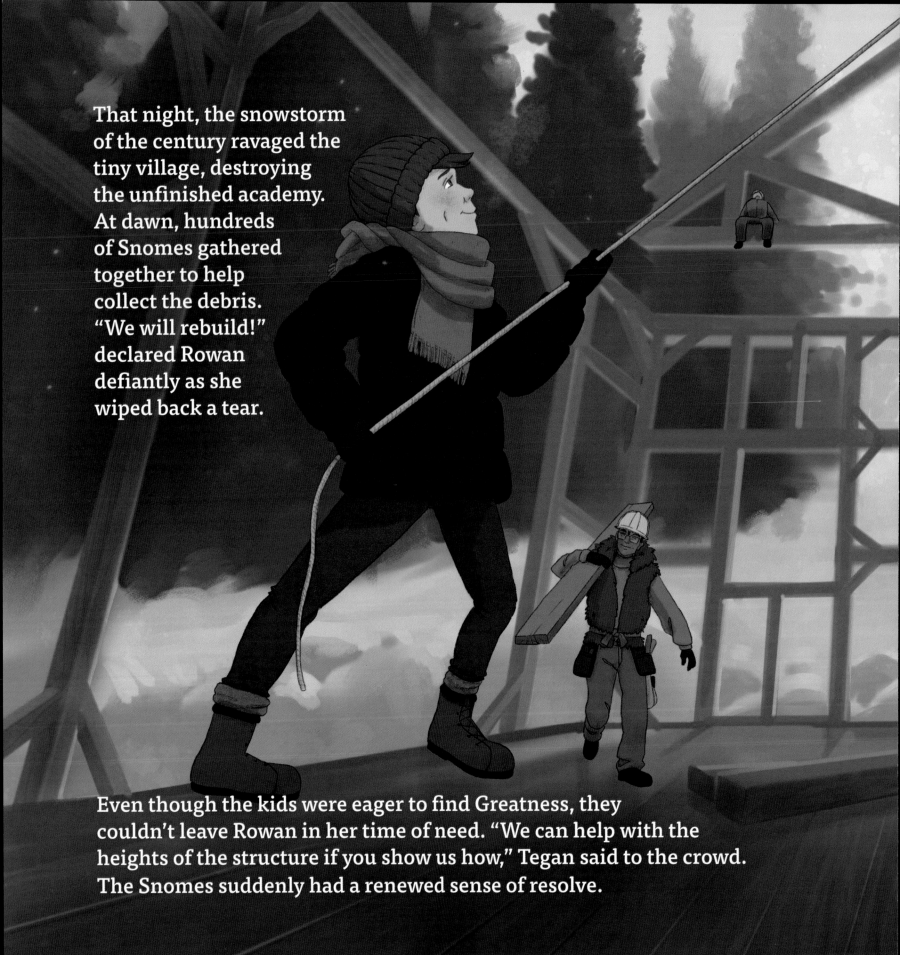

That night, the snowstorm of the century ravaged the tiny village, destroying the unfinished academy. At dawn, hundreds of Snomes gathered together to help collect the debris. "We will rebuild!" declared Rowan defiantly as she wiped back a tear.

Even though the kids were eager to find Greatness, they couldn't leave Rowan in her time of need. "We can help with the heights of the structure if you show us how," Tegan said to the crowd. The Snomes suddenly had a renewed sense of resolve.

Once again, hammers were put to nails as walls were framed and lifted. Soon the roof trusses were set as the building took shape in record time.

After doing everything they could to help, the kids knew it was time to move on. Leaving the village, the thankful Snomes called out to them, "We believe in you."

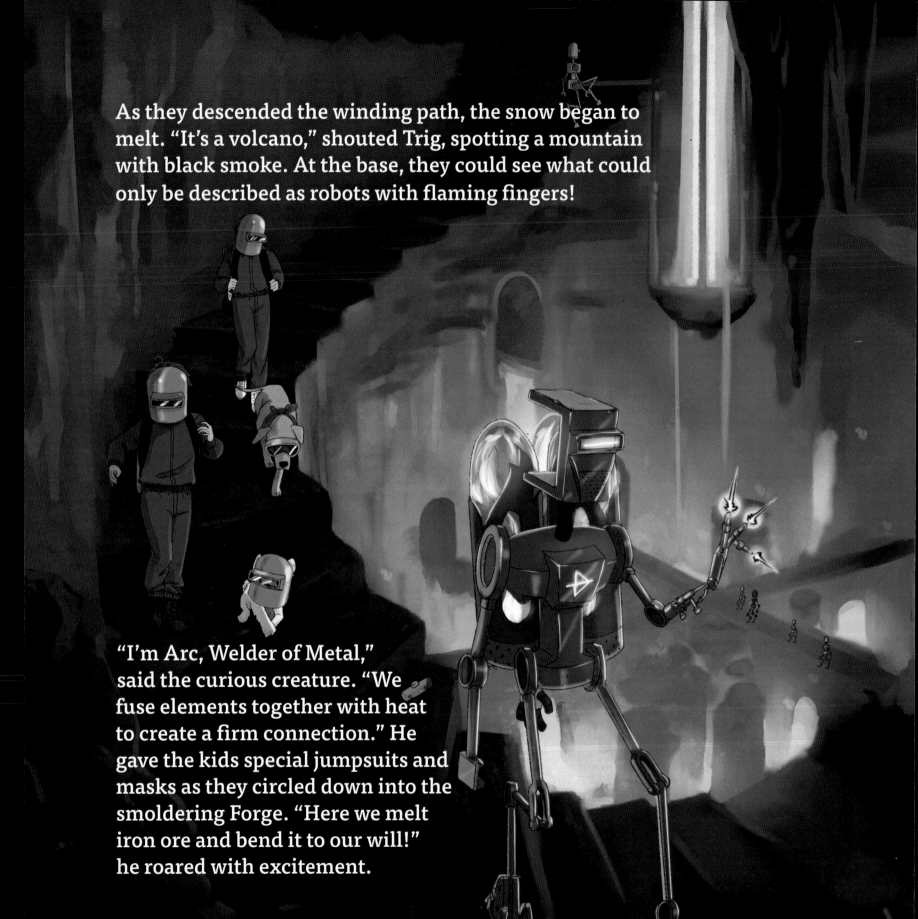

As they descended the winding path, the snow began to melt. "It's a volcano," shouted Trig, spotting a mountain with black smoke. At the base, they could see what could only be described as robots with flaming fingers!

"I'm Arc, Welder of Metal," said the curious creature. "We fuse elements together with heat to create a firm connection." He gave the kids special jumpsuits and masks as they circled down into the smoldering Forge. "Here we melt iron ore and bend it to our will!" he roared with excitement.

Arc and the kids followed the Forgers as they carried cooled steel beams to a staging area near a steep canyon. "We're building a bridge to cross the ravine," Arc said.

Sure enough, that was the way to Greatness with no bridge yet to cross. The kids felt defeated. Trig tried to remind Tegan. "Don't give up now, Greatness can't be far!" He turned to Arc. "Can we help finish the bridge?"

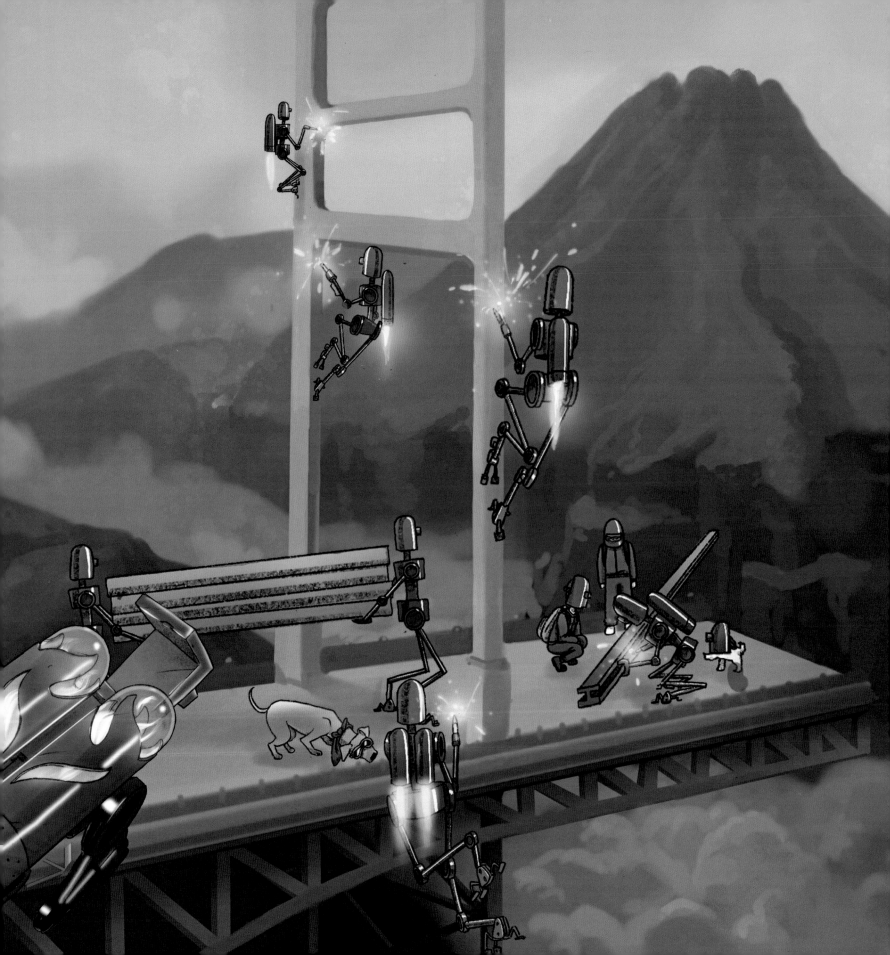

In the shadow of the volcano, they learned about the welding process. Some workers lifted steel beams using huge cranes as welders sat atop the bridge, sparks flying from their fingers as they joined the metal across the expanse.

Finally, the day arrived when the bridge connected, allowing the kids to cross the gap for the first time. Arc and the Welders waved from the foot of the span, shouting, "WE BELIEVE IN YOU!"

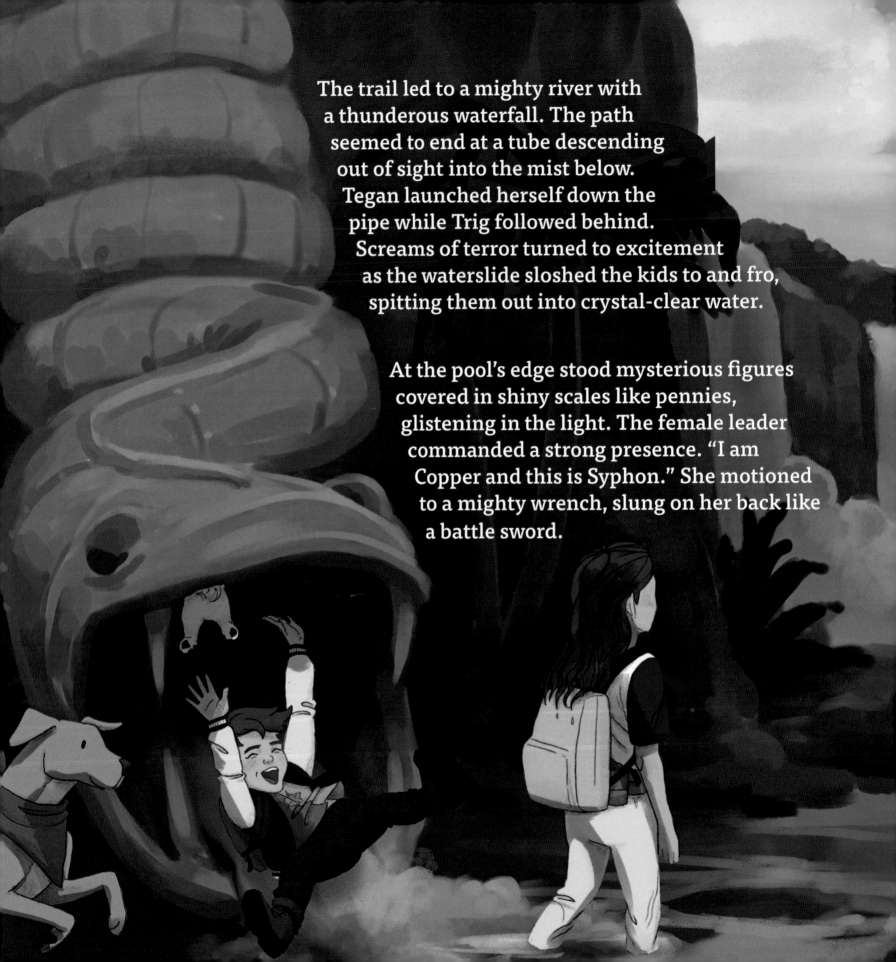

The trail led to a mighty river with
a thunderous waterfall. The path
seemed to end at a tube descending
out of sight into the mist below.
Tegan launched herself down the
pipe while Trig followed behind.
Screams of terror turned to excitement
as the waterslide sloshed the kids to and fro,
spitting them out into crystal-clear water.

At the pool's edge stood mysterious figures
covered in shiny scales like pennies,
glistening in the light. The female leader
commanded a strong presence. "I am
Copper and this is Syphon." She motioned
to a mighty wrench, slung on her back like
a battle sword.

As she spoke, a fountain behind her began to bubble.
"We're plumbers who study the ancient art of fluid dynamics.
We've helped villages grow into big cities by knowing how
gravity, pressure, and water work together."

"Do you know the way to Greatness?"
Tegan asked.

Copper smiled and said, "Follow me." She led them down a maze of tubes crisscrossing into the horizon. At the final slide, they came across a chaotic scene of water spewing from a severed pipe. Copper sprang into action as she shut the valve. "A tree fell and crushed the connection," she determined. Copper withdrew Syphon from her back as her eyes flashed. "I love a good challenge."

Inspired, the kids learned from the plumbers as they reconnected the pipe using clamps, seals, and couplings. Lastly, Copper used the jaws of Syphon to secure the pipe, making the final connection. The siblings reopened the valve, allowing water to flow once more.

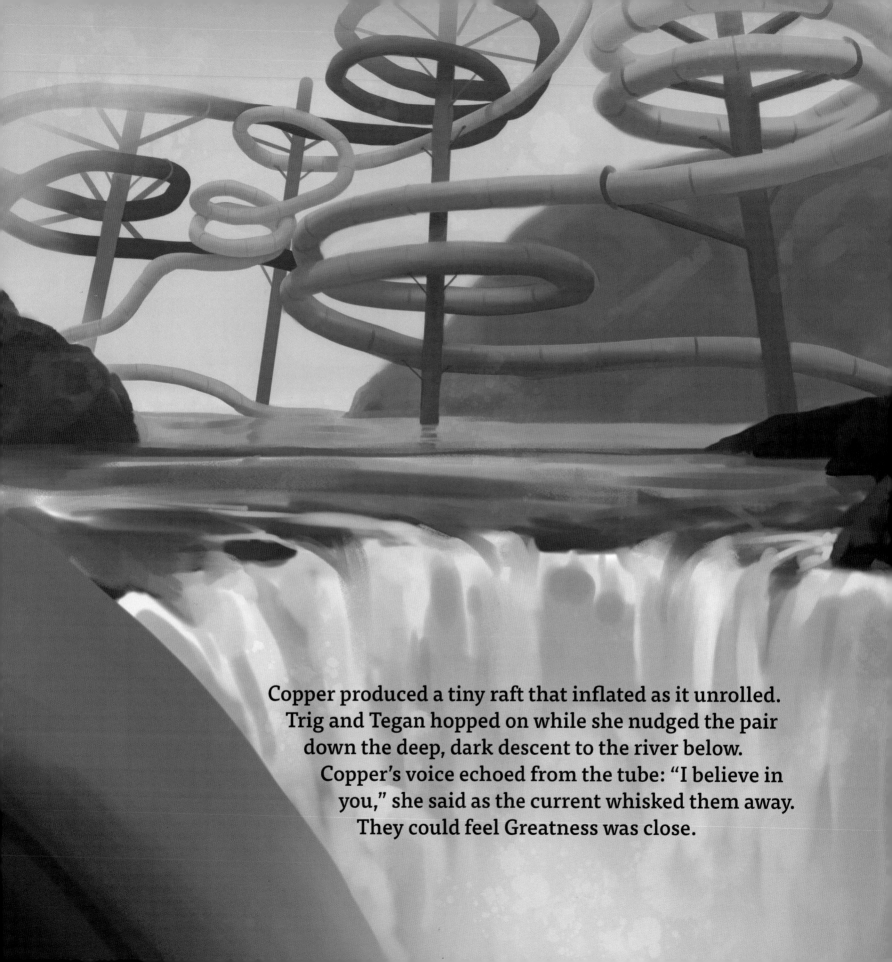

Copper produced a tiny raft that inflated as it unrolled.
Trig and Tegan hopped on while she nudged the pair
down the deep, dark descent to the river below.
Copper's voice echoed from the tube: "I believe in
you," she said as the current whisked them away.
They could feel Greatness was close.

Flashes of light cracked across the dark sky. Carved into the mountainside were the longest, steepest steps. Cautious but confident, the kids left the raft and began climbing higher. Pushing through the clouds, their hair stood on end as two enormous red doors began to open.

At the entrance, a figure wearing a long coat and a glowing meter radiating from his chest stood with arms extended.
As they stepped inside, Tegan asked,
"Are you a wizard?"

"I am the Electrician Magician," he said.
"I conduct electricity to do wondrous
and powerful things. You thought
the doors opened by magic, eh?
But the fact is, they're operated
by a motion sensor!"

A futuristic tram emerged on a track,
taking the trio on a fast-moving ride along
large circuits as power surged through a giant
grid. "Electricity changed the world!"
cried the Electrician Magician.

The large cavern funneled to a narrow opening. "I can take you to Greatness," said the Electrician Magician, "but we must first light the way." Tegan and Trig stared into the dark tunnel. There was no option but to help.

Day in and out, the Electrician Magician taught them the importance of grounding and showed them how to measure resistance while pulling wire, hanging light fixtures, and energizing circuits.

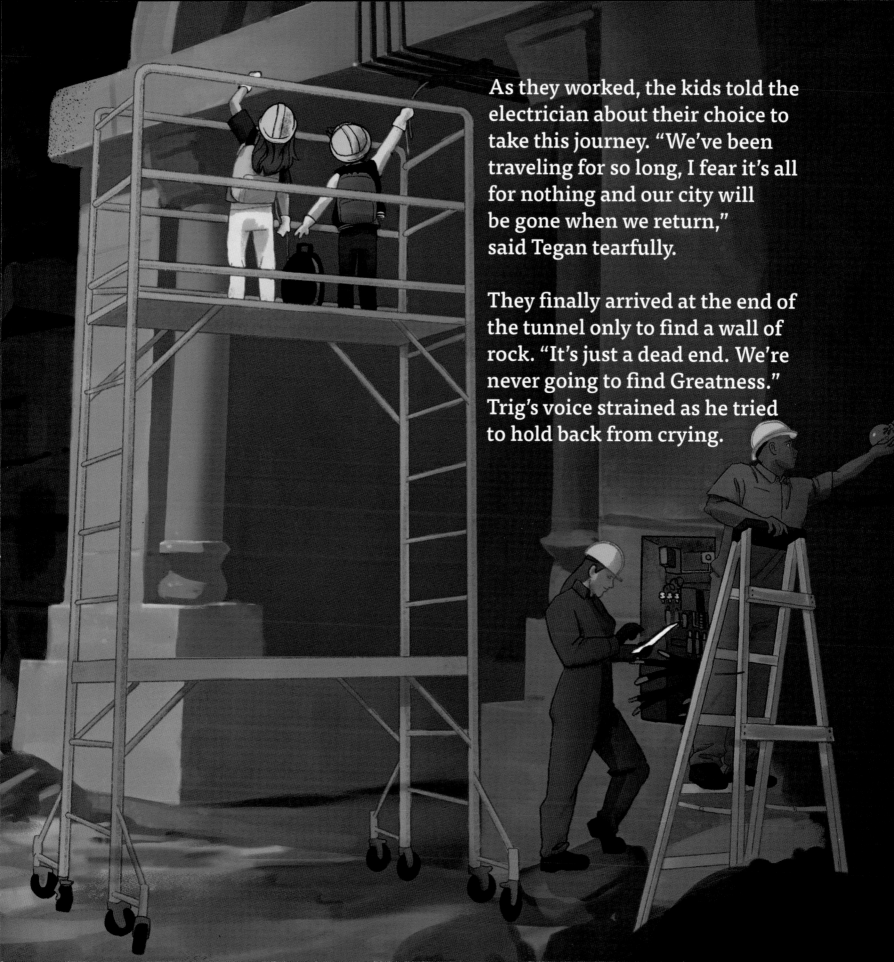

As they worked, the kids told the electrician about their choice to take this journey. "We've been traveling for so long, I fear it's all for nothing and our city will be gone when we return," said Tegan tearfully.

They finally arrived at the end of the tunnel only to find a wall of rock. "It's just a dead end. We're never going to find Greatness." Trig's voice strained as he tried to hold back from crying.

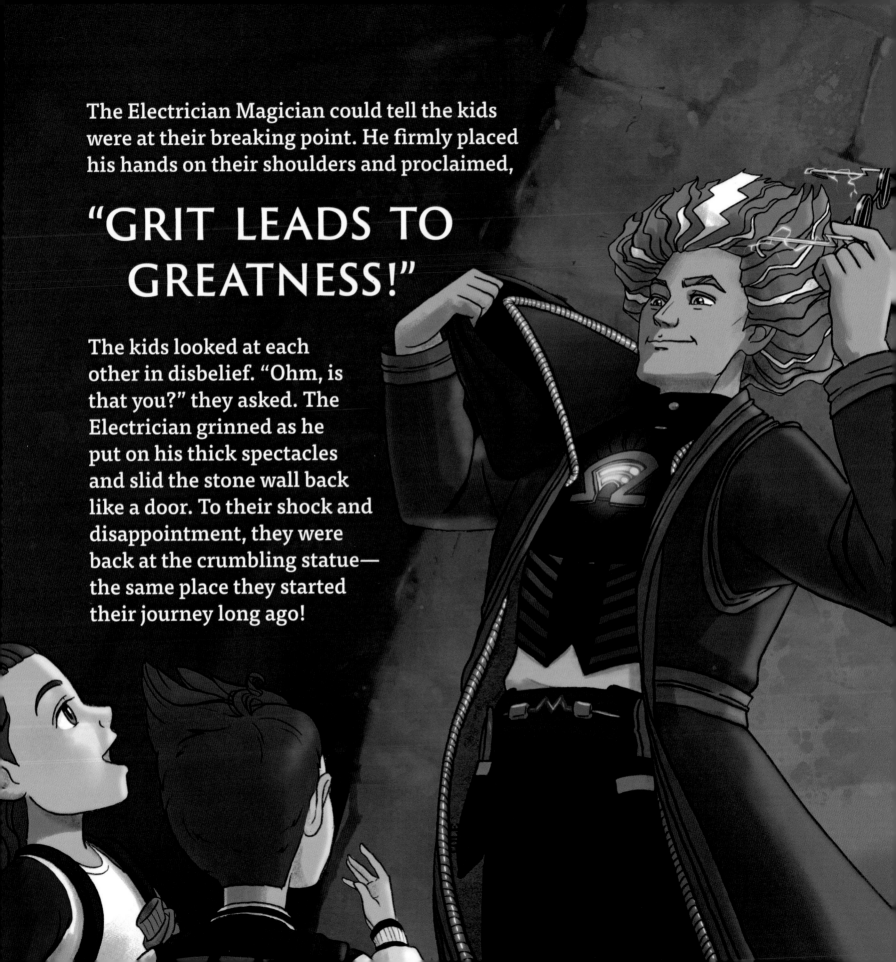

The Electrician Magician could tell the kids were at their breaking point. He firmly placed his hands on their shoulders and proclaimed,

"GRIT LEADS TO GREATNESS!"

The kids looked at each other in disbelief. "Ohm, is that you?" they asked. The Electrician grinned as he put on his thick spectacles and slid the stone wall back like a door. To their shock and disappointment, they were back at the crumbling statue—the same place they started their journey long ago!

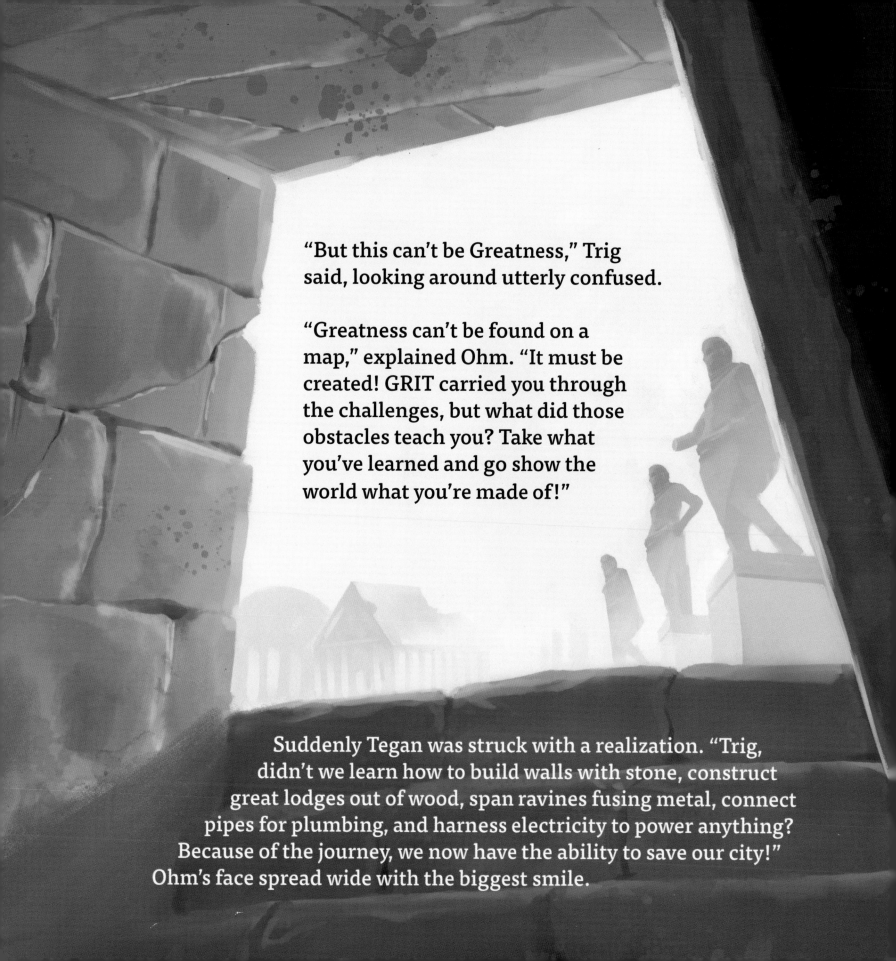

"But this can't be Greatness," Trig said, looking around utterly confused.

"Greatness can't be found on a map," explained Ohm. "It must be created! GRIT carried you through the challenges, but what did those obstacles teach you? Take what you've learned and go show the world what you're made of!"

Suddenly Tegan was struck with a realization. "Trig, didn't we learn how to build walls with stone, construct great lodges out of wood, span ravines fusing metal, connect pipes for plumbing, and harness electricity to power anything? Because of the journey, we now have the ability to save our city!" Ohm's face spread wide with the biggest smile.

Out of the tunnel emerged the trade friends that had believed in them all along: Mason the Mason, Rowan the Carpenter Snome, Arc the Welder, and Copper the Plumber with Syphon behind her back.

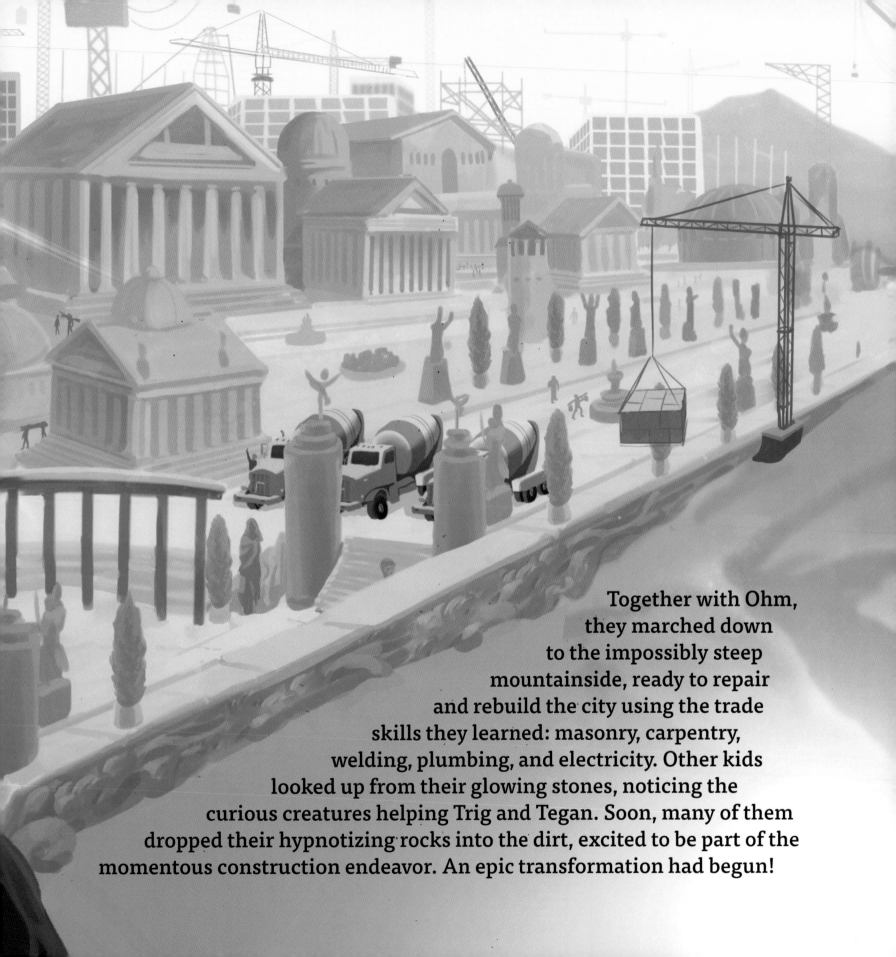

Together with Ohm,
they marched down
to the impossibly steep
mountainside, ready to repair
and rebuild the city using the trade
skills they learned: masonry, carpentry,
welding, plumbing, and electricity. Other kids
looked up from their glowing stones, noticing the
curious creatures helping Trig and Tegan. Soon, many of them
dropped their hypnotizing rocks into the dirt, excited to be part of the
momentous construction endeavor. An epic transformation had begun!

Once the city was saved from disaster, its citizens held a grand parade to celebrate their incredible achievement. The heroes wore grass crowns and the sky rained with flowers as massive crowds unified at the city center. There before them towered polished statues where crumbling monuments once stood. Beyond the statues emerged two new ones: not men and women of old, but two kids with grass crowns. It was Tegan and Trig!

Trig's eyes lit up as he noticed the newly chiseled inscriptions. "Tegan! It looks like we found Greatness after all!"

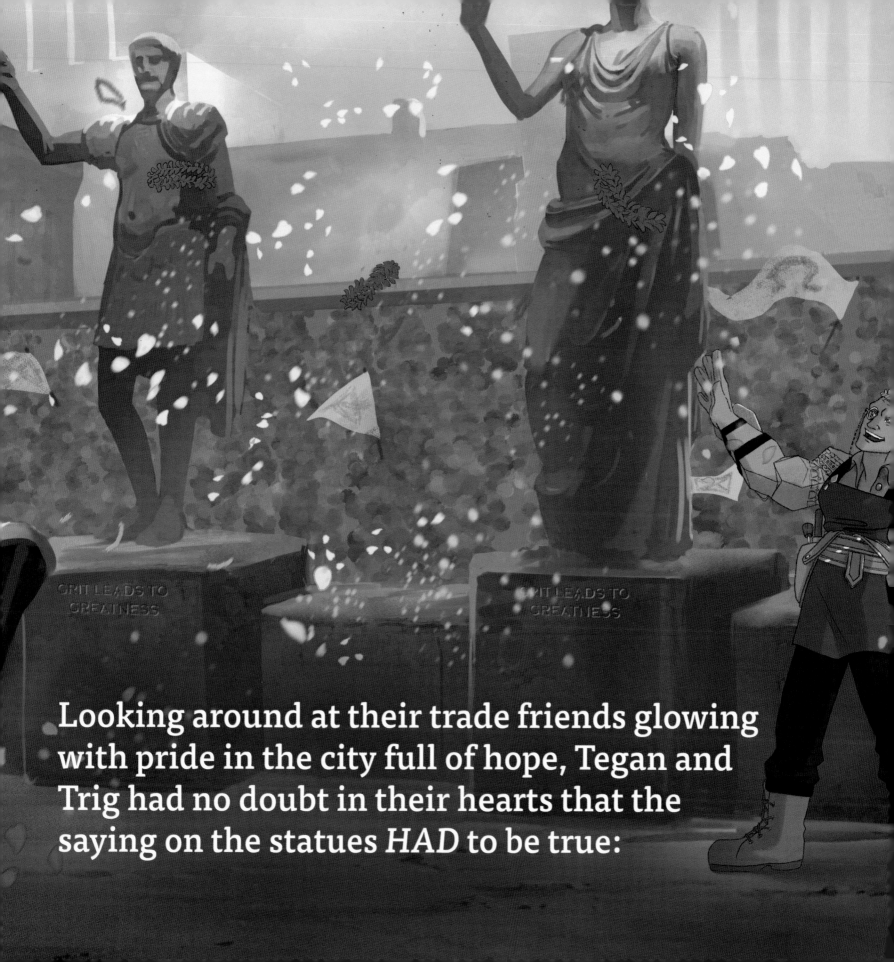

Looking around at their trade friends glowing with pride in the city full of hope, Tegan and Trig had no doubt in their hearts that the saying on the statues *HAD* to be true:

GRIT LEADS TO GREATNESS

GRIT LEADS TO
GREATNESS

GRIT LEADS TO
GREATNESS

ABOUT THE AUTHORS

Jenny Kerr Schroen

Jenny Kerr Schroen grew up in a creative, close-knit family in Northern Kentucky near Cincinnati, Ohio. She attended the University of Kentucky and later pursued graphic design at Flagler College in St. Augustine, Florida. She spent the next fifteen years exploring the world, practicing design, and travel blogging with her sisters. Deciding life wasn't wild enough, she reconnected with and married J.D., a widowed college friend, who had four young children. Jenny moved cross-country from California to reside in Salisbury, Maryland, with her new instant family. She later became the Creative Developer for Delmarva Veteran Builders (DVB), a commercial construction firm. In 2020, she won a MarCom Award, an international creative competition, for developing DVB's ad campaign "*Grit Leads to Greatness*". In-depth research regarding the power of GRIT and her first-hand view of the workforce shortage inspired Jenny to co-write the children's book, *Grit Leads to Greatness*, a nod to her own children for persevering through tough times while demonstrating to all people the vital impact construction trades have on the world.

:camera: *JauntingJenny*

Chris Eccleston

Chris Eccleston is the CEO and founder of Delmarva Veteran Builders (DVB) located in his hometown of Salisbury, Maryland. He proudly served in the navy for six years as a nuclear machinist mate, completing three tours overseas. After the military, Chris received a construction management degree from the University of Maryland Eastern Shore and an MBA from Salisbury University. He is an epic believer in his wife, Kennan, and their two children. Being in the construction industry for over fifteen years, he has seen firsthand the decline in interest in the trades. He has become a passionate warrior defending the image of tradespeople. His goal is to inspire the next generation into the trades and serve as a beacon for parents and educators, highlighting the purpose and impact a career in construction can provide. As DVB grew, the company gained recognition for its strong company culture and fresh approach. Chris has always been creative-at-heart, possessing a long-time vision to write a children's book about construction.

in *Christopher Eccleston*

MEET THE ILLUSTRATORS

Justin Donaldson

Justin Donaldson is an Australian freelance artist and art instructor living in South Carolina with his wife and children. He is greatly inspired by nature and is known for communicating those feelings of peace and wonder through epic fantasy landscapes.

www.JustinDonaldsonArt.com  Justin_Donaldson_Art

Rachel Danae

Rachel Danae is a freelance illustrator and Justin's assistant and mentee. Her personal work combines the beautiful chaos of nature with themes of comfort, friendship, and adventure.

MakeTheHappy